OUTRAGEOUS, BODACIOUS, CONTAGIOUS . . . AND JUST PLAIN GROSS

What would Joey Buttafucco be if he went to Harvard?

A Kennedy.

What's the nicest thing you can say to a girl from Alabama?

"Nice tooth."

What's the difference between a Polish woman and a catfish?

One has whiskers and smells bad. The other is a fish.

Why is aspirin white?

Because it works.

What's the best thing about having Alzheimer's?

You can hide your own Easter eggs.

GROSS JOKES

by Julius Alvin

AWESOMELY GROSS JOKES	(0-8217-3613-2, $3.50)
AGONIZINGLY GROSS JOKES	(0-8217-3648-5, $3.50)
INTENSELY GROSS JOKES	(0-8217-4168-3, $3.50)
INFINITELY GROSS JOKES	(0-8217-4785-1, $3.99)
TERRIBLY GROSS JOKES	(0-8217-4873-4, $3.50)
SAVAGELY GROSS JOKES	(0-8217-5149-2, $4.50)

OUTRAGEOUSLY GROSS JOKES

Julius Alvin

Zebra Books
Kensington Publishing Corp.

http://www.zebrabooks.com

ZEBRA BOOKS are published by

Kensington Publishing Corp.
850 Third Avenue
New York, NY 10022

First Printing: November, 1997
10 9 8 7 6 5 4 3 2 1

Printed in the United States of America

For Paul Dinas

You've been a wonderful audience

Contents

Now That's Gross!

This truck driver was speeding through a small country town and ran over a big rooster. He appeared at the first farm he came to and knocked on the door. A farmer's wife answered. "What do you want?" she asked.

"Ma'am," the trucker said, "I would like to replace your rooster."

The farmer's wife looked him up and down. "Let me see your manhood, mister," she said.

The truck driver was confused, but showed her his pecker.

"Fair enough," the farmer's wife replied. "The chickens are out back."

What's the best thing about getting a blow job?

The five minutes of silence.

"I don't understand," Joe complained to his friend. "People take an instant dislike to me the moment I tell them I'm a lawyer. Why is that?"

"Maybe it just saves time."

What's the difference between politics and a wife?

Politics suck.

The lonely secretary is walking home from work one day when she spots a strange-looking bottle on the side of the road. She picks it up and dusts it off, unleashing a genie.

"I grant you one wish," the genie says.

The homely girl thinks about it. She says to the genie, "I'm a virgin. When I get home, I'd like to see my cat turned into a handsome young hunky guy."

"So shall it be," the genie booms and disappears back into the bottle.

The secretary rushes home and finds a tall, handsome stud in her apartment. He rips her clothes off and carries her into the bedroom, laying her on the bed. He kisses her and nuzzles her neck until she's ready to explode with passion.

"Oh, take me, take me now," she gasps.

"I would, but you had me neutered last month."

How do you know you're really getting old?

There are twelve candles on your piece of birthday cake.

What do you call a black woman who practices birth control?

A humanitarian.

What do you call diarrhea in Mississippi?

A brain drain.

Why are peckers like Calvin Klein jeans?

It takes a lot of yanks to get them off.

When a Puerto Rican leaves the U.S., he says "Farewell." When he comes back, he says "Welfare."

Why did the 80-year-old woman stop wearing her belt?

Every time she tried to tighten it, her tits got in the way.

What's the definition of a meat substitute?

A dildo made from soybeans.

Bill Gates and Steven Spielberg have lunch together at a fancy Beverly Hills bistro. Afterwards, they're walking along Rodeo Drive and pass a Rolls Royce dealership.

Bill Gates inspects the sticker on the window of one Rolls and says, "Seventy-five grand. I think I'll buy it."

"No, let me, Bill," Spielberg says. "You paid for lunch."

Two men are on death row, scheduled to die on the same night. The warden asks each one if he has any last requests.

The first inmate says, "Yes, Warden. I'd like to hear 'Achy Breaky Heart' one last time before I die."

The warden says to the second inmate, "Do you have a last request?"

"Yes. Kill me first."

Gross Gay and Lesbian Jokes

How does a fag know when spring has arrived?

A gerbil comes out of his ass and doesn't see its shadow.

What's the difference between a fag and a refrigerator?

A refrigerator doesn't fart when you pull the meat out.

What present did the fag hairdresser want for his birthday?

To be teased and blown.

Hear about the gay midget?

He came out of the cupboard.

What's the definition of an anal suppository?

A chastity belt for fags.

What's the definition of GAY?

Got Aids Yet?

What's the difference between a fag and a suppository?

About four inches.

Why were gay men the first ones to leave town when the earthquake struck?

They already had their shit packed.

What do a male hustler and a lawyer have in common?

They both make their living fucking people up the ass.

Why did the San Francisco Police Department fire the gay detectives?

Because they blew all their cases.

Why do fags act like such pricks?

You are what you eat.

What do you call a fag who's into bondage and discipline?

A sucker for punishment.

What's the definition of confusion?
A blind lesbian in a fish market.

Why did the fag get fired from the Hershey plant?

He didn't pack enough fudge.

What's the definition of an open can of sardines?

Lesbian potpourri.

Hear about the gay burglar?

He couldn't blow the safe, so he went down on the elevator.

Why do gay men grow mustaches?

To hide their stretch marks.

Really Offensive Ethnic Jokes

Why do Polish women have breast enlargements?

So they don't have to pay a flat tax.

The Polish farmer says to his neighbor, who is carrying a burlap bag over his shoulder, "Hey, Stan, if I guess how many chickens you got in that bag, can I have one?"

His neighbor says, "I don't need them. You can have them both."

The Polack says, "All right. There's five."

How come there are no black workers at Microsoft?

They won't do WINDOWS.

Carmine the bookie passes away suddenly. All of his Italian friends and customers from his Brooklyn neighborhood show for the funeral.

The priest steps up to the pulpit to deliver the eulogy. "Remember this," he says, "Carmine isn't dead, he's sleeping in that sweet land of Eternity."

"I seen Carmine's body," comes a rough voice from the back of the chapel. "A hundred bucks says he's dead."

What's Tupac spelled backwards?

Caput.

What do you call a rapper who dies in a drive-by shooting?

A rap hit everyone can enjoy.

How did the FBI break up the Million Man March?

They dropped job applications from helicopters.

How do you know when a Polack has robbed your house?

The dog is pregnant and the garbage cans are empty.

Why do black people always kill each other?

Who cares?

What's the worst thing you can say to a Mexican?

"Be yourself."

What's the difference between a rich Jew and a poor Jew?

A poor Jew has to wash his own Mercedes.

Why aren't there any dogs in the Vatican?

They like to piss on Poles.

What's the Italian definition of "bigamist?"

A very dense fog bank.

So Epstein, after three very hard years, graduates from law school with honors. Since he's never been laid in his twenty-four years, he decides to spend all his money going to a whorehouse. Trouble is, he's only got nine dollars. He goes to the whorehouse anyway.

The madam says to him, "I've got this gorgeous blond, just flew in from Stockholm. She's yours for fifty dollars."

Epstein says, "I'm sorry, but I couldn't afford that."

The madam says, "No problem. I've also got a nice Polish girl. Only thirty dollars."

Epstein says, "I'm sorry, but I can't afford her."

"Okay, how about a black gal for ten dollars."

Epstein tells the madam, "I'm sorry. I've only got nine dollars."

The madam thinks about it for a minute, then says, "All right. Nine dollars is nine dollars. I'll take you on myself."

Epstein has sex with the madam and goes away happy.

Eighteen years go by. Epstein is now a successful lawyer, worth a few million, and has a beautiful wife and family. Life is good. Then, one afternoon, the old madam shows up at his office, with a teenage boy in tow.

The madam says to Epstein, "Do you remember me?"

Epstein says, "No, I don't think I do."

The madam says, "Eighteen years ago, you

came to my whorehouse. You only had nine dollars, so I took you on myself." She points to the teenage boy. "This is your son."

Epstein is nobody's fool.

He writes out a check for $30,000 and signs it "Alvin Epstein." He hands it to the boy.

"Alvin Epstein?" he says. "You mean I'm a lousy Jew?"

"Don't complain, kid. Another buck and you'd have been a nigger."

A monkey and a black man are sitting in a tree. What do you call the black man?

The assistant branch manager.

How many pieces does a Polish jigsaw puzzle have?

One.

The Jew says to the genealogist, "How much would it cost to trace my family tree back to the old country?"

"Five thousand dollars," she tells him.

"Too much," the Jew says. "Is there any way to do it cheaper?"

"Yeah," she says. "Try running for President."

A Polack comes to New York City on vacation. He goes into a fancy bar-restaurant and runs up a bill of one hundred dollars.

"This is outrageous," the Polack complains. "Back in Poland, you can drink as much as you want without paying. You can sleep in the finest hotels for free and when you wake up in the morning, there's fifty dollars on the pillow next to you."

"Give me a break," the bartender says. "Has that ever actually happened to you?"

"No, not really," the Polack says. "But my wife says it happens all the time."

The Polack comes home from work one night and is stopped by his neighbor, who tells him, "It may be none of my business, but this afternoon a strange man came to your house and your wife let him in. I peeked through the blinds and I saw them making passionate love."

The Polack asks, "Was he tall, about six feet?"

The neighbor answers, "Yes, I think he was."

"Did he wear glasses and have red hair?" the Polack asks.

"Yes," the neighbor agrees.

"Then that was just the mailman," the Polack responds. "He'll fuck anyone!"

Why did the black farmer try to breed an octopus with a chicken?

So everyone in his family could have a leg.

What did the sign at the movie theater in Alabama say?

"CHILDREN UNDER THIRTEEN NOT ADMITTED UNLESS ACCOMPANIED BY THEIR HUSBANDS."

How do you know when you're truly living in Alabama?

You get married for the third time and you still have the same in-laws.

How do you know you're *really* living in Alabama?

You have a home that's mobile and ten cars in the front yard that aren't.

How do you know when you're at a Polish wedding?

The groom is wearing a clean bowling shirt.

What are a Jewish baby's first words?

"Trust fund."

Five Italians are playing poker, as they do every Friday. At midnight, Louie comes back from the bathroom and says to their host, "Hey, Nick, I just seen Guido makin' love to your wife in the kitchen."

"Okay, that's it, guys," Nick says. "This is positively the last deal."

After the wedding, Marie is taken upstairs by the groom, Tony. Five minutes later, Marie comes running downstairs into the kitchen, where her mother is making tea.

"Mama," Marie exclaims. "Tony, he's gotta hair all over his chest."

"He's-a supposed to have hair on his chest," Mama says. "You go back-a upstairs."

Five minutes later, Marie comes charging back into the kitchen.

"Mama, Mama," Marie cries. "Tony, he's-a gotta hair on his legs."

"He's-a supposed to have the hair on the legs," Mama says, "You go back-a upstairs."

There, Tony takes off his shoes and socks, revealing a clubfoot.

Marie runs back into the kitchen and declares, "Tony, he's only a halfa foot."

Mama's eyes light up. She says to her daughter, "You stay-a here. I'm-a going upstairs."

Why did the Polish butcher fall behind in his work?

He backed into the meat grinder.

What's a Puerto Rican vacation?

Hanging out on the neighbor's stoop with a six-pack.

What do you call it when a Jew farts in a blizzard?

A kosher cold cut.

In a Word, Sex

How do they define safe sex in Montana?

Branding the sheep that kick.

A couple checks into the most expensive hotel in Paris. They order up room service—a cozy dinner for two. The room service waiter sets out the meal, then asks, "Will there be anything else?"

The husband replies, "No, thank you."

The waiter asks, "And for your wife?"

The husband thinks for a moment and says, "Yes. Call her and tell her I'll be home the day after tomorrow."

"I don't think my wife loves me anymore," the worried husband says to his shrink.

"How can you tell?" the shrink asks.

"Well, when I come home from work, she greets me at the door with a nice dry martini. Then she cooks me a great dinner. Later, when we go to bed, she lets me do all kinds of kinky things to her and she never objects."

"So what's the problem?"

"Maybe I'm being overly sensitive, but when she thinks I'm asleep, she whispers in my ear, 'Die you lousy son of a bitch, die!' "

What's a politician's idea of safe sex?

No press.

What do you call a rock star with PMS?

John Cougar Menstrual-cramp.

Two old men are sitting in Central Park. Max says to Sam, "So congratulate me. I'm getting married again."

"Married? Max are you crazy? You're ninety-two years old."

"So sue me, I'm in love."

"Can she cook?" Sam wants to know.

"She can't even boil water."

"Is she pretty at least?" Sam asks.

"She's got a face like a horse."

"Is she, maybe, good in bed?"

"Good in bed?" Max snorts. "She's two years older than me and hasn't done it in thirty years."

"Then why the hell are you marrying her?"

"She can drive at night."

What's the difference between oral sex and Christmas?
At Christmas, it's better to give than to receive.

Why wasn't Heidi Fleiss handcuffed when she was arrested by the L.A. police?

It would have cost an extra $500.

The wife of a Hell's Angel goes to see a fortune teller.
"Prepare to be a widow," the fortune teller says, gazing into her crystal ball. "Your old man is going to die very, very soon."
"Yeah, I know. But will I be acquitted?"

A tourist gets lost in the back woods of Alabama. He comes upon a broken-down mobile home out in the middle of nowhere. Two rednecks are sitting in lawn chairs out front. The tourist asks them directions back to the interstate. They tell him. Before he leaves, though, he asks one of the rednecks, "What do you boys do for fun out here?"

"Well," the first redneck says, "mostly what we do for fun is hunt and kill and fuck."

"What do you hunt and kill?"

"Something to fuck."

Two old whores are watching a parade. The first one starts to cheer and wave the American flag.

"I just love soldiers," she says.

"Yeah, yeah," her friend says. "You say that every war."

The old geezer says to his physician, "Doc, I just don't have any interest in sex anymore."

The doctor asks, "How old are you, Jake?"

Old Jake replies, "Ninety-six."

The doctor tells him, "Exactly. Face it, Jake, you're not getting any younger. At your age, a man's bound to see a decrease in his sexual drive. When did you first notice that you were losing interest in sex?"

Jake says, "Twice last night, and then again this morning."

A worried husband says to the psychiatrist, "Doctor, I don't know what to do. My wife thinks she's a lawn mower!"

"That's terrible," the psychiatrist says. "Why didn't you bring her to see me sooner?"

"I tried, but my neighbor wouldn't return her."

Twelve-year-old Timmy comes home from school. His mother asks him, "Did you learn anything today?"

Timmy says, "We learned all about sex education. About penises and vaginas and stuff."

Timmy's mother is shocked. She says, "Is that what they're teaching you in school nowadays? I'm going to complain to the principal!"

"Relax, Mom," Timmy assures her. "This is the nineties. It's all a part of what they call higher education."

Timmy goes up to his room. An hour or so later, his mother calls him down to dinner. When he doesn't respond, she goes upstairs to his room. Timmy is laying on his bed, jerking off.

"Timmy, when you're done with your homework, supper's on the table."

Why do blonds use pencil on their eyebrows?

They have to draw the line somewhere.

Why is marriage like a tornado?

There's a lot of sucking and blowing, but when it's over, you always lose your house.

What's the definition of a loser?

A guy who tries to get laid at a family reunion.

A Miscellaneous Variety

This young female intern is working at a nursing home. She meets Mrs. Schwartz, who is ninety-nine years old. The intern starts examining Mrs. Schwartz, who asks the pretty young doctor, "Are you married, sweetheart?"

"Yes," the female intern replies. "My husband and I have been married for a year."

Mrs. Schwartz asks her, "Any children yet?"

"My husband is a stockbroker and I'm hoping to become a doctor. We just don't have the time to have children."

"Time, shmime," Mrs. Schwartz snorts. "My husband and I had six children. We have sixteen grandchildren, ten great-grandchildren, and the whole thing took only fifteen minutes!"

"So how's your husband?" Annie's mother asks her daughter.

"Not so good, Mom," Annie says. "He cut his finger on a bread knife and he's in the hospital for two weeks."

"That seems like a long time for a simple cut," Annie's mother says. "Have you seen the doctor?"

"No," Annie replies. "But I've seen the nurse."

Why did God create businessmen?

To make weathermen look good.

So the candidate for governor says to his constituents, "I promise to lower taxes, reduce illegal immigration, and clean up dirty politics."

A man in the crowd says, "You're a lying sack of shit!"

"Yes, I am," the politician says. "Just let me finish."

A man goes to his doctor because he's having trouble breathing. The doctor takes a look up the man's nose and gasps.

The doctor says to his patient, "Did you know you have cauliflower growing in your nose?"

That's terrible, doc," the patient says. "I planted marijuana!"

What's the difference between Johnny Cochran and Divine Brown?

At least Johnny Cochran got his client off.

What do you get when you mix fifty lesbians with fifty politicians?

One hundred people who don't do dick.

What's the difference between a money launderer and a congressman?

Once in awhile, a money launderer passes a few good bills.

What did the loser do before the cockfight?

He greased his zipper.

So the guy says to his virgin bride on their wedding night, "Now that we're married, sweetheart, I don't want you to feel any pressure when it comes to making love. When you're in the mood for sex, yank on my penis once."

"What if I'm not in the mood for sex?" the bride asks.

"Then yank it a hundred times."

What's the definition of wicker box?

What Elmer Fudd wants to do to Madonna.

What's the definition of a hysterectomy?

When you remove the nursery but leave the playpen.

What did the first psychiatrist say to the second psychiatrist when they met on the street?

"You're fine. How am I?"

What do you get when you cross a rooster and a chick who works for AT&T?

A cock that wants to reach out and touch someone.

Hear about the Polack who couldn't spell?

He spent the night in a warehouse.

Where do masochists have lunch?
At a smack bar.

Why did the Japanese leper commit suicide?

Because he lost face.

What's the best thing about having Alzheimer's?

You can hide your own Easter eggs.

What are the last three words a man wants to hear when he's making love?

"Honey, I'm home."

What's green and has an IQ of 160?

A platoon of marines.

Tom can't decide which of his three girlfriends he wants to marry, so he gives them a test. He gives them each five thousand dollars and tells them to spend it any way they want.

The first girlfriend spends it on a new wardrobe and tells him, "I wanted to look really nice so you'd want to marry me."

The second girlfriend takes the five thousand and refurnishes the boyfriend's apartment. She says, "I wanted you to have a nice place for when we get married."

The third girlfriend invests her five thousand on Wall Street and turns it into $50,000. She says, "I wanted to make money for us so we could have a great honeymoon and buy a house."

Which girlfriend did the guy marry?

The one with the biggest tits.

So this couple goes out on a blind date and halfway through dinner the guy decides he can't take another minute. He excuses himself to go to the bathroom, then seeks out his waiter and says, "Call me to the telephone when I get back to the table."

The waiter does and the guy excuses himself and goes to the phone. He comes back to the table and says to his date, "I'm sorry, but I've got to leave. My grandmother just died."

"Thank God," his date says. "If yours hadn't, mine was about to."

Mrs. O'Brien goes to see the family doctor. She asks him for a remedy to give her husband more sexual stamina.

The doctor hands Mrs. O'Brien a bottle of pills and tells her, "Give your husband one of these each evening and give him a shot of whiskey, too."

A few weeks later, Mrs. O'Brien goes back to see the doctor, who asks her how things are working out.

"Well," she says, "My husband is behind on the pills, but he's six months ahead on the whiskey."

What's the definition of real pain?

Jumping off the Empire State Building and catching your eyelid on a nail.

What's the definition of a lesbian?

A woman trying to do a man's job.

What do you get when you breed a cat and a rabbit?

A pussy hare.

What's the definition of love?

The myth that one cunt is different from another cunt.

What's the name of the airline for senior citizens?

Incontinental.

Why did the ninety-year-old man hire a nanny?

Because he wanted to be Pampered.

What's another name for Harlem?

"Scene of the crime."

Now That's Sick!

What's the definition of conceit?

A flea with a hard-on who asks, "Had enough yet, bitch?"

Hear about the guy who dropped his wallet in San Francisco?

He had to kick it all the way to Los Angeles before he could pick it up.

What do you call a guy who's brain-dead, has no arms and legs, and a twelve-inch cock?

Partially disabled.

So Harry is two hours late for work. His boss says, "This is the last straw, Harry. You come in late again without a good excuse, your ass is fired."

Two days later, Harry comes in four hours late. The boss says, "Okay, Harry, I said I'd fire you again if you didn't have a good excuse, so it better be good."

"Oh, it's good," Harry replies. "See, I was walking to work, right along the railroad tracks like I always do. And what do I see tied to the tracks but the sexiest damn woman I've ever laid eyes on. Well, I untied her and banged the shit out of her all morning."

"Yeah?" the boss asks. "Did she give you any head?"

"Nah," Harry says. "I couldn't find it."

How do you get twenty Mexicans into a phone booth?

Tell them they own it.

How many surrealists does it take to screw in a lightbulb?

Fish.

So an Italian walks into a bar and orders a martini. He looks down at the end of the bar and sees a guy who looks very familiar.

"Hey," the Italian says, "ain't that Jesus Christ over there?"

"As a matter of fact, it is Jesus Christ," the bartender says.

"I'd like to buy Him a drink," says the Italian.

The bartender gives Jesus Christ a martini. Jesus acknowledges it with a nod and a smile.

A few minutes later, a Polack walks into the bar and orders a beer and a shot. He says to the bartender, "That looks like Jesus Christ!"

"It is Jesus Christ," says the bartender.

The Polack likewise buys Jesus Christ a drink. Jesus acknowledges it with a nod and a smile.

A few minutes later, a black guy comes into the bar and orders a bourbon and soda. He says to the bartender, "Man, is that Jesus Christ?"

"Yes, it is," the bartender says.

The black guy buys Jesus Christ a drink. Jesus acknowledges it with a nod and a smile.

Ten minutes later, Jesus gets up to leave. On the way out, he puts his hand on the Italian's shoulder and says, "Thank you for the drink, my son."

"It's a miracle!" the Italian says. "I had arthritis and was in pain all the time, but your hand has healed me completely!"

Jesus then walks up to the Polack, puts his hand on his shoulder, and thanks him.

The Polack exclaims, "I had a pinched nerve in my neck and was in pain all the time, but now I'm healed!"

Jesus walks over to the black guy.

"Yo, man, don't be touching me," the black guy says. "I'm on disability."

What's the recipe for chicken à la Vietnam?

First, napalm a chicken coop, then . . .

What's the difference between Maine and New Hampshire?

In New Hampshire, Moosehead is a beer. In Maine, it's sexual assault.

Two Polish terrorists are driving through the streets of Krakow on their way to blow up an embassy. "Hey, Stosh," the first Polack asks, "what happens if that bomb we got in the back-seat blows up before we get there?"

"Don't worry," the second Polack replies. "I've got another one in the trunk."

Why don't Italians barbecue?

The spaghetti keeps falling through the grill.

How do you know when you live in a really bad neighborhood?

The church has a bouncer.

How do you know when you're in a Harlem high school?

The school newspaper has an obituary page.

So the young yuppie husband and wife both get downsized and are flat broke. The only way to make money, the husband decides, is for his wife to work the streets.

So the first night, a car stops on the wife's corner. The john asks her, "How much for straight sex?"

"Just a minute," the wife says, and runs over to where her husband is waiting. "How much should I charge for straight sex?" she asks him.

"Tell him a hundred bucks," the husband says.

She runs back to the waiting john and says, "One hundred bucks."

The john says, "I don't have a hundred. How much for a hand job?"

She runs back to her husband and asks him how much she should charge for a hand job. "Forty bucks," he tells her.

The john agrees to her price and proceeds to pull out a twelve-inch cock.

"Wait a minute," she tells the john, and rushes back to her husband. "Honey," she asks, "can we lend that nice man sixty dollars?"

So the Jewish guy comes home early from work one day. As he pulls up, he sees a plumber's truck in the driveway.

"Please Lord," the husband prays, "let her be having an affair!"

What did Jesus say to Mary when he was on the cross?

"Can you get me my flats? These spikes are killing me."

What did one unemployed yuppie say to the other?

"There's no such thing as a free brunch."

So the racist loses his job as a furniture salesman and joins the police force. His first week on the job, he kills a dozen drug dealers, bank robbers, and other assorted criminals, all of them black.

"So, how's the job coming?" the new cop's best friend asks one day.

"Just great," the racist says. "What I like best about it is, the customer is always wrong."

How do you know Jesus Christ wasn't really born in Italy?

Three wise men and a virgin? Come on.

Gross Celebrity Jokes

Why did Kato Kaelin wear tennis shoes to the O.J. trial?

He heard there was going to be recess.

What's the difference between John and Lorena Bobbitt?

She's crazy and he's just nuts.

What did Bill Clinton tell Hillary after sex?

"I'll be home in twenty minutes."

So Newt Gingrich, Bob Dole and Bill Clinton find themselves in the land of Oz. They follow the Yellow Brick Road and meet the Wizard, who grants each of them one request.

Gingrich asks for a brain. He gets one.

Dole asks for a heart. He gets one.

Clinton asks the Wizard, "Is that girl Dorothy still around?"

What did Woody Allen say to Michael Jackson?

"I'll give you two tens for a twenty."

What's the definition of saturated fat?

Rush Limbaugh in a hot tub.

Bumper sticker of the month: "If Clinton is the answer, it was probably a stupid question."

What do you get when you cross Dr. Kevorkian, Dr. Ruth, and Tonya Harding?

Drop-dead sex that will bring you to your knees.

What's the best thing about living next door to a Hare Krishna?

You can always get a free ride to the airport.

What's the difference between O.J. Simpson and Pee Wee Herman?

It only took ten jerks to get Pee Wee off.

What do you call a Deadhead who just broke up with his girlfriend?

Homeless.

Hear about the new Bill Clinton golf ball?

It's guaranteed a perfect lie every time.

How did Bill Clinton slow down inflation?

He handed it over to the post office.

Hear about the new Marilyn Monroe stamp?

When you lick it, you feel just like a Kennedy.

What did Bob Hope do on Labor Day?

He entertained the troops guarding the White House.

How do you know when your house has been robbed by a Deadhead?

Your thongs are missing.

Why did Michael Jackson quit the Cub Scouts?

He was up to a pack a day.

Hear about the new Heidi Fleiss doll?

When you buy one, she gets you another doll.

Why did they take John Wayne toilet paper off the market?

It wouldn't take shit from anyone.

So the very attractive woman spots a man in the elevator with her and he looks familiar.

She says, "Aren't you Donald Trump?"

"As a matter of fact, I am," Trump replies.

"I think you're great," the woman says. "How would you like to go back to my room? I'll give you a blow job you'll never forget, and then I'll fuck you six ways from Sunday."

"I don't know," Trump replies. "What's in it for me?"

What does "Magic" stand for?

"My Ass Got Infected, Coach."

Why doesn't Roseanne ever go to the beach?

Because the Greenpeace people keep pushing her back into the ocean.

How did Jim Bakker meet Tommy Faye?

They were both dating Jimmy Swaggart.

What's the Spanish word for Rodney King?

Piñata.

A Gross Variety

What are the three best things about women?

They bleed without cutting themselves.
They can bury a bone without digging a hole.
They can make a man come without calling.

Jake and Sam are sitting on a park bench. Sam says, "So Jake, how's the wife?"

"To tell you the truth," Jake replies, "I think she's dead."

Sam is shocked. He says, "How can you say such a thing? What do you mean she's dead?"

"Well," Jake says, "The sex is the same, but the dirty dishes are piling up in the sink."

What do you call making love to a porcupine?

Prickly heat.

What do you call a midget circumcision?

A Tiny Trim.

What's the definition of eternity?

The hour when you come and she leaves.

How do you know when you're really getting old?

You're with a woman all night long and the only thing that comes is the dawn.

Why is it bad when a blond has PMS?

It stands for Permanent Mental State.

What's the difference between an in-law and an outlaw?

An outlaw doesn't want to live in your guest room.

What's the definition of pile carpeting?

Hair on hemorrhoids.

What's the best way to find a whore who gives golden showers?

Follow the yellow brick road.

What's the definition of gross?

Getting a hard-on and running out of skin.

What's the difference between men and women?

Women play hard to get; men get hard to play.

How do you drown a blond?

Tell her not to swallow.

Why did the girl leave the convent?

She found out that *nun* really means *none.*

When is it time to stop screwing doggie style?

When your girlfriend starts chasing cars.

So one woman boasts to her best friend, "I have two boyfriends, and I've never been happier. One is handsome, kind, caring, and considerate."

"Then what do you need a second one for?"

"Because he's straight."

How many Hollywood agents does it take to screw in a lightbulb?

Ten—but they'll accept eight.

So the guy goes to his doctor. The guy's cock is covered with green and purple spots.

"My God," the doctor exclaims. "How did that happen?"

"I don't exactly know, doc," the guy says. "I was driving down 42nd Street when I spotted this gorgeous blond hooker. I made love to her all night and then a week later, this." He points to his multicolored cock. "What should I do?"

"Next time take 34th Street."

What's the definition of an optimist?

An accordion player with a beeper.

What's another definition of an optimist?

A promiscuous queer who buys an IRA.

Why do men swim faster than women?

They have a built-in rudder.

What do you call a mountain climber who just had a vasectomy?

Dry sack on the rocks.

What's the true purpose of toilet paper?

Film for your brownie.

So the doctor says to the husband, "I think we can cure your sexual dysfunction. But it's very expensive."

"How expensive?" the husband asks.

"Well, one procedure is $15,000 and is seventy percent effective. The second procedure is $20,000 and is one hundred percent effective. So here's what I suggest," the doctor continues. "Go home and discuss it with your wife, then come back when you've made your decision."

Two days later, the husband comes back. The doctor asks him, "Which procedure have you decided on?"

"Neither," the husband replies. "We decided to remodel the kitchen instead."

So Joe and Eddie are having some beers. Something is troubling Eddie, Joe can tell. After a lot of prodding, Eddie finally blurts out, "Okay, the trouble is your wife."

"My wife?" Joe asks. "What about her?"

"I think she's cheating on us."

How do you get twenty yuppies into a minivan?

Promote one and watch the other nineteen climb up his ass.

What do you call a lesbian with fat fingers?

Well hung.

What's a typical WASP ménage à trois?

Two headaches and a hard-on.

The newlyweds were uncomfortable using the word *sex,* so they agreed to refer to their lovemaking as "doing the laundry." This went on for years, even after their children were born.

One day the husband felt in the mood and sent his young son downstairs to ask his wife if she wanted to do the laundry. Fifteen minutes passed, then a half hour, then an hour and a half. Finally the kid came back and told his father, "Mommy says she'll do the laundry in five minutes."

"Tell her not to bother," the father said. "Tell her it was a small load and I did it myself."

More
Really Sick Jokes

What do you call two women in a freezer?

Cold cunts.

"The man next to me is jerking off!" cries the girl to her friend in the dark movie house.

"Just ignore him," her friend says.

"I can't. He's using my hand."

What happens when a girl puts her panties on backwards?

She gets her ass chewed out.

What's the definition of an overbite?

When you're eating pussy and it tastes like shit.

What are brownie points?

Things you find in a Brownie's bra.

What's oral sex in Chinese?

Tung chow.

What's oral sex with an unhygienic Chinese girl?

Tung chow yuk.

What's the definition of a lap dog?

An ugly girl who gives great head.

What's a Chinese guy with constipation?

Hung dung.

So Phil goes to the barbershop for a haircut. The barber points to a curly blond hair in Phil's mustache. "Where'd that come from?"

Phil says, "Oh that? Every morning before I leave I give my wife a kiss on the head."

"Okay," the barber says. "Thing is, you've got shit all over your necktie."

What's the difference between a pussy and a cunt?

A pussy is soft and warm and inviting . . . and a cunt is the one who owns it.

What's the difference between eating sushi and eating pussy?

The rice.

What do you call a blond between two brunets?

A mental block.

Why are Italian hookers so busy?

They never let a dago by.

What's the definition of a moron?

A guy who thinks his wife is going to church when she comes home with a Gideon bible.

What would Joey Buttafucco be if he went to Harvard?

A Kennedy.

Hear about the priest who gave up drinking?

It was the longest ten minutes of his life.

What do you call a German with a hard-on?

A frau-loader.

So Murray is romping in bed with a married woman when they hear the garage door open.

"It's my husband," the frantic woman cries. "Get out of bed and start ironing these." She tosses a bunch of shirts at him.

The husband strolls in and asks his wife about the strange man ironing shirts.

"He's our new housekeeper," the wife says.

Her husband seems to accept the explanation. Murray stays and finishes ironing the shirts. Later, he leaves and walks to the corner to catch the bus. He can't help but start bragging about his narrow escape and relates his experience to a man waiting next to him at the bus stop.

The man says to Murray, "Are you talking about the redhead who lives in the brick house over there?"

"Yes, I am," Murray admits.

"Hell, son," the man says. "I'm the one who *washed* the shirts."

What's the definition of artificial insemination?

A technical knock-up.

What's Helen Keller's favorite mouthwash?

Jergen's hand lotion.

What's the difference between a girlfriend and a toothbrush?

You don't let your friends borrow your toothbrush.

What happens when a straight man walks into a gay bar for the first time?

He feels a little queer.

What's the definition of a Jewish "10"?

A girl with two tits and eight million dollars.

Why do blonds like cars with sunroofs?

There's more leg room.

What happened to the leper when he walked into the screen door?

He strained himself.

So Goldberg says to Cohen, "My wife and I took a class in efficiency."

"Why did you do that?" Cohen asks.

"Well," Goldberg says, "I noticed my wife's routine at breakfast for years. She made dozens of trips between the stove, refrigerator, and the table, always carrying one dish at a time. So we took this class."

"Did it help?"

"It sure did. It used to take her twenty minutes to put breakfast on the table. Now it only takes me seven."

What did the flasher say to the woman in Alaska?

"It's really cold. Mind if I just describe myself?"

What's the definition of henpecked?

A husband who is sterile, afraid to tell his pregnant wife.

The prisoner is escorted by two guards to the conference room at the jail, where his attorney is waiting.

"Sam," the prisoner says, "you gotta get me out of here."

"Jack, don't worry," the lawyer says to his handcuffed client. "Everything's cool. Even if I can't prove to the jury that you were out of town on the night of the triple murder, I have two shrinks who'll testify that you were insane. Just in case, I'll pay off all of the district attorney's witnesses. Also, the judge is a good friend and he owes me one, big time."

"That's great," the prisoner says. "What do I need to do?"

The lawyer says, "Just to be safe, try and escape."

How do you know when your lawyer is well hung?

You can't get your fingers between his neck and the noose.

What's the difference between McDonald's and a black prostitute?

McDonald's has only served 100 million.

What do you get when you cross a black man and an ape?

A monkeyshine.

What do you call a retired black prostitute?

Grandma.

So a cop in Harlem sees an old black woman kicking a can down the street. He says to her, "What are you doing?"

"I'm moving," she says.

What do you call a Puerto Rican vampire?

Spicula.

What happened when the two queers got into an argument?

They exchanged blows.

What do you call a baby before it's born?

Daddy's little squirt.

Why is a Jewish divorce so expensive?

Because it's worth it.

What was the most popular item at the Cajun-Polish restaurant?

Blackened toast.

How can you tell when a pirate is Polish?

He has eye patches over both eyes.

What do you get when you cross Arnold Schwarzenegger and a Jew?

Conan the Wholesaler.

Hear about the Italian inflatable doll?

Put a ring on her finger and her hips expand.

How do you know when a Jew is really cheap?

He can't even pay attention.

How can you tell when the bride at a Jewish wedding is really ugly?

Everyone lines up to kiss the caterer.

What do you call a black woman who's had three abortions?

A crime buster.

What do you call a woman who's lost most of her intelligence?

Divorced.

How many feminists does it take to change a lightbulb?

Fourteen. Six to form a Women's Lightbulb Changing Committee, and eight to protest that changing lightbulbs is exploitation of women.

What do you call a gay lumberjack?

Spruce.

So a rabbi and a priest are walking down the beach in Miami. Suddenly, a sea lion walks past them, followed by a naked woman. Then, ten mice stroll into a restricted country club, followed by two Italians carrying pizzas.

Seeing this, the priest turns to the rabbi and opens his mouth to speak.

"Forget it, Father," the rabbi says. "I've already heard this one."

Why do blonds smile when they see lightning?

They think they're getting their picture taken.

Why don't women have brains?

Because they don't have dicks to put them in.

Why do men cut holes in their pants pockets?

So they can run their fingers through their hair.

What's the difference between a beer and a piss?

About twenty minutes.

How do you know when a black woman reaches orgasm?

The next guy on line taps you on the shoulder.

What do you call a blond with no arms, no legs, and no torso?

Muffy.

What's the definition of a really great nurse?

A woman who makes the patient without disturbing the bed.

Why is sodomy so easy?

Any asshole can do it.

What's the definition of a perfect marriage?

Your housekeeper and your wife both come a couple of times a week.

Why don't blonds eat bananas?

They can't find the zippers.

What's the best way to train your girlfriend to give oral sex?

Tie her hands behind her back and make her eat spaghetti.

Why do fags love hamburgers?

Because it's hot meat between two nice buns.

Not Politically Correct Gross Jokes

How do you know when you're living in Alabama?

You fart in public and blame it on your dog.

What's the nicest thing you can say to a girl from Alabama?

"Nice tooth."

How do you know when you're really in the south?

You go to a wedding reception at Denny's.

What's one definition of a loser?

A guy who gets blacklisted by a bowling alley.

So the woman calls the town psychiatrist and cries, "Doctor, you've got to come over right away. My husband's in really bad shape."

The shrink rushes over. The worried wife says, "Thank God you're here, doctor. Just go down the hall. He's in the last room on the right."

The shrink goes into the room and sees the woman's husband sitting on the edge of the bathtub, dangling a fishing line in the toilet.

He goes back to the wife and says, "Yes, this is very serious. Why didn't you call me sooner?"

"Who had time?" the wife asks. "I've been cleaning fish all week."

What did one dog say to the other dog when they saw a parking meter for the first time?

"Look, Rover—a pay toilet."

What's a mixed marriage in San Francisco?

Partners of the opposite sex.

So six-year-old Billy says to his best friend Andy, "My daddy his two dicks."

"Have you seen 'em?" Andy asks.

"Sure," Billy says. "He uses one to pee with and the other to brush the baby-sitter's teeth."

What's the definition of alimony?

A man's cash surrender value.

What's the difference between a dog and a dick?

A dog stops coming when you beat it.

Where does virgin wool come from?

Really ugly sheep.

How do you know when you're from Georgia?

Your car breaks down on the side of the road and you never go back to get it.

What's another way of knowing you're from Georgia?

You think people who have electricity are snobs.

What's another?

You know how to milk a goat.

Why do dogs stick their noses in blonds' crotches?

Because they can.

What's the difference between two lawyers in a BMW and a porcupine?

A porcupine has his pricks on the outside.

Why was the ninety-year-old man acquitted of rape?

The evidence wouldn't stand up in court.

Two Polacks are standing on the street corner, watching a dog lick his balls.

"I sure wish I could do that," the first Polack says.

"You better ask the dog first," the second Polack says.

How do Polacks count to ten?

One . . . two . . . three . . . then another . . . then another . . ."

What's the best thing about having a female president?

You don't have to pay the bitch as much as a man.

Hear about the Polack who went ice fishing and came home with twenty pounds of ice?

His wife died trying to fry it.

What did Helen Keller say when she picked up a matzo?

"This is good. Who wrote this?"

"Grandpa, Grandpa," little Joey says. "Can you croak like a frog?"

"I guess so," Grandpa says. "Why do you ask?"

"Cause Mommy says that when you croak, we're all going to Disney World!"

What's the difference between sex for money and sex for free?

Sex for free costs a lot more.

So the gay guy checks into the hospital to have an operation. The morning after, the surgeon goes to see the patient.

"So how are we doing this morning?" the surgeon asks.

"Okay, doctor. I just have one question: When can I . . . you know . . . resume a normal sex life?"

"I'm not sure," the surgeon says. "You're the first one to ask after a tonsillectomy."

What's the definition of "indefinitely?"

You're indefinitely when your balls are slapping her ass.

So the gynecologist came home from work and slumped into a chair.

"Tired, dear?" his wife asked.

"Honey, I'm bushed."

Why is aspirin white?

Because it works.

How do you make a woman scream twice?

Fuck her up the ass then wipe your dick on her blouse.

"Mommy, Mommy," little Joey asks. "Where do babies come from?"
"The stork," Mommy says.
"I know," Joey says. "But who fucks the stork?"

What does NRA really stand for?

Nigger Removal Agency.

What do you get when you cross an agnostic and a Jehovah's Witness?

Someone who knocks on your door for no reason.

What's the difference between a Polish woman and a catfish?

One has whiskers and smells bad. The other one is a fish.

Why don't Bosnians go out to bars anymore?

They get bombed at home.

How does a Greek firing squad line up?

One behind the other.

So the Polack leaves the bar drunk out of his mind. Despite the bartender's protests, the Polack tries to drive home.

Less than a mile away, he gets pulled over by a cop.

"What seems to be the problem, occifer?" the Polack asks the cop drunkenly.

"Good evening, sir," the cop says. "Drinking?"

The Polack says, "You buying?"

"Doctor," Epstein says, "my wife is driving me crazy. I have to get rid of her. What can I do?"

"Take these pills," the doctor says. "Give her one a day then screw her six times. In a month it will kill her."

A month later, Epstein shows up in the doctor's office in a wheelchair, looking thirty years older.

"My God," the doctor exclaims. "What happened to you?"

"It's okay, Doc," Epstein says. "In another two days she'll be dead."

Why do men have bigger brains than dogs?

So they don't hump women's legs at parties.

What does a faggot get after he's been gang-raped?

A full moon.

What does Sinead O'Connor do after she combs her hair?

Pulls her pants up.

What's the difference between a Jewish American Princess and a pit bull?

A nose job and a mink coat.